Kindergarten, Here We Come!

by Quinlan B. Lee
illustrated by Ana Bermejo

Scholastic Inc.

ISBN 978-0-545-94860-9

10 9 8 7 6 5 4 3 2   16 17 18 19 20
Printed in the U.S.A.   40

First printing 2016
Book design by Carla Alpert

Hannah, Sam, Zara, and
Leo are in pre-K.

The kids have been pals all year.
But the year is almost over.

It is time to get ready for kindergarten!

The class sits on the rug for circle time.
"Today is a big day," says Ms. Bird.
"It is Kindergarten Sneak Peek Day!"

"Yay!" says Sam.
"I like to sneak."
"I like to peek!" says Hannah.

7

Leo raises his hand.
"What is Sneak Peek Day?"
he asks.

Kindergarten
Sneak Peek Day

Ms. Bird smiles.
"Today we are going to visit kindergarten.
You will see how big and fun it is!"

"Is there story time in kindergarten?" asks Zara.

"Yes," says Ms. Bird.
"There is story time in kindergarten."

"Are there desks in kindergarten?" asks Leo.
"Yes, there are big desks," says Ms. Bird.

"Are there books in kindergarten?"
asks Sam.
"I love books!"

"Yes," says Ms. Bird.
"There is a library full of books!"

"Is there art in kindergarten?"
asks Zara.
"Yes," says Ms. Bird.
"You can draw and paint in
kindergarten."

"What about lunch?" asks Leo.
"Do we eat lunch in kindergarten?"

"Yes," says Ms. Bird.
"You will eat in a big lunchroom."

Sam waves his hand.
"Is there a slide in kindergarten?"
he asks.

"Yes," says Ms. Bird.
"There is a big slide in kindergarten."

"There are kids in kindergarten, too," says Ms. Bird.
"Big kids!
And there are new friends."

"I like new friends," says Hannah.
"But I don't like big kids."

"Yes, you do," says Ms. Bird. "Let me show you."

Stand Tall Wall

Hannah goes to the Stand Tall Wall.
"Look how you grew this year,"
says Ms. Bird.

"My turn!" says Sam.

Ms. Bird smiles.
"Sam, you grew this much.
Your hair grew, too!"

"So who are the big kids in kindergarten?" Ms. Bird asks.

The pre-K pals smile.
"We are the big kids!" Leo says.

"That's right," says Ms. Bird.

"You are big kids now!
You are ready for kindergarten."

"Kindergarten, here we come!" Zara says.